In Loving Memory of Mama Nora — M.D.R.

And special thanks to
Charlotte Nesbitt, Assistant Coordinator
for the Douglass Branch Library;
Barbara McGee, Douglass Annex Supervisor;
Monica Jones and the Douglass Double Dutchers;
and Alice for her patience and understanding — M.D.R.

Cover design: Like many colonial women of their time, African-American women made quilts to preserve history and record family memories. Sometimes, using only scraps of cloth and a needle and thread, these artists magically wove history and family memories into cloth much like a storyteller, using only his or her voice, would weave history and memories into a story that could be told by future generations.

In the past, quilts were handed down from one generation to the next. The stories depicted on the quilts literally covered each generation as they slept, binding them together by common memories.

Today, seeking to preserve this ageless folk art, Melodye Rosales has designed her own quilt for the cover of *Double Dutch and the Voodoo Shoes.* She has intricately woven characters and events into the quilt that reflect the mood and feelings of the story.

Adventures in Storytelling

Double Dutch and the Doodler Shoes

From an Original Story by Warren Colman

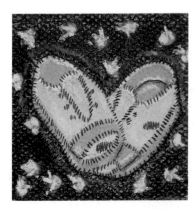

Illustrated by Melodye Rosales

CHILDRENS PRESS ®
CHICAGO

Adventures in Storytelling

Dear Parents and Teachers,

Adventures in Storytelling Books have been designed to delight storytellers of all ages and to make world literature available to non-readers as well as to those who speak English as a second language. The wordless format and accompanying audiocassette make it possible for both readers and nonreaders who are unacquainted with a specific ethnic folktale to use either the visual or the audio portion as an aid in understanding the story.

For additional reference the complete story text is printed in the back of the book, and post-story activities are suggested for those who enjoy more participation.

The history of storytelling

"Once upon a time . . . ."

"Long ago but not so long ago that we cannot remember . . . ."

"In the grey, grey beginnings of the world . . . ."

"And it came to pass, more years ago than I can tell you . . . ."

These are magic words. They open kingdoms and countries beyond our personal experiences and make the impossible possible and the miraculous, if not commonplace, at least not unexpected.

For hundreds of years people have been telling stories. You do it every day, every time you say, "You'll never believe what happened to me yesterday"; or "You know, something like that happened to my grandmother, but according to her, it went something like this . . . ."

Before video recorders, tape recorders, television, and radio, there was storytelling. It was the vehicle through which every culture remembered its past and kept alive its heritage. It was the way people explained life, shared events, and entertained themselves around the fire on dark, lonely nights. The stories they told evoked awe and respect for tradition, ritual, wisdom, and power; transmitted cultural taboos and teachings from generation to generation; and made people laugh at the foolishness in life or cry when confronted by life's tragedies.

As every culture had its stories, so too did each have its storytellers. In Africa they were called griots; in Ireland, seanachies; in France, troubadours; and in the majority of small towns and villages around the world they were simply known as the gifted. Often their stories were hundreds of years old. Some of them were told exactly as they had been told for centuries; others were changed often to reflect people's interests and where and how they lived.

With the coming of the printing press and the availability of printed texts, the traditional storyteller began to disappear — not altogether and not everywhere, however. There were pockets in the world where stories were kept alive by those who remembered them and believed in them. Although not traditional storytellers, these people continued to pass down folktales, even though the need for formal, professional storytelling was fading.

In the nineteenth century, the Grimm brothers made the folktale fashionable, and for the first time collections of tales from many countries became popular. Story collections by Andrew Lang, Joseph Jacobs, and Charles Perrault became the rage, with one important difference: these stories were written down to be read, not told aloud to be heard.

As the nineteenth century gave way to the twentieth, there was a revival of interest in storytelling. Spearheaded by children's librarians and schoolteachers, a new kind of storytelling evolved — one that was aimed specifically at children and connected to literature and reading. The form of literature most chosen by these librarians and teachers was the traditional folktale.

During this time prominent educator May Hill Arbuthnot wrote that children were a natural audience for folktales because the qualities found in these tales were those to which children normally responded in stories: brisk action, humor, and an appeal to a sense of justice. Later, folklorist Max Luthi supported this theory. He called the folktale a fundamental building block, an outstanding aid in child development, and the archetypal form of literature that lays the groundwork for all literature.

By the middle of the twentieth century, storytelling was seen as a way of exposing children to literature that they would not discover by themselves and of making written language accessible to those who could not read it by themselves. Storytelling became a method of promoting an understanding of other cultures and a means of strengthening the cultural awareness of the listening group; a way of creating that community of listeners that evolves when a diverse group listens to a tale well-told.

Many of these same reasons for storytelling are valid today — perhaps even more relevant than they were nearly one hundred years ago. Current research confirms what librarians and teachers have known all along — that storytelling provides a practical, effective, and enjoyable way to introduce children to literature while fostering a love of reading. It connects the child to the story and the book. Through storytelling, great literature (the classics, poetry, traditional folktales) comes alive; children learn to love language and experience the beauty of the spoken word, often before they master those words by reading them themselves.

Without exception, all cultures have accumulated a body of folktales that represent their history, beliefs, and language. Yet, while each culture's folktales are unique, they also are connected to the folktales of other cultures through the universality of themes contained within them. Some of the most common themes appearing in folktales around the world deal with good overcoming evil; the clever outwitting the strong; and happiness being the reward for kindness to strangers, the elderly, and the less fortunate. We hear these themes repeated in stories from quaint Irish villages along the Atlantic coast to tiny communities spread throughout the African veldt and from cities and towns of the industrialized Americas to the magnificent palaces of the emperors of China and Japan. It is these similarities that are fascinating; that help us to transcend the barriers of language, politics, custom, and religion; and that bind us together as "the folk" in folktales.

Using wordless picture books and audiocassettes

Every child is a natural storyteller. Children begin telling stories almost as soon as they learn to speak. The need to share what they experience and how they perceive life prompts them to organize their thoughts and express themselves in a way others will understand. But storytelling goes beyond the everyday need to communicate. Beyond the useful, storytelling can be developed into a skill that entertains and teaches. Using wordless picture books and audiocassettes aids in this process.

When children hear a story told, they are learning much about language, story structure, plot development, words, and the development of a "sense of story." Wordless books encourage readers to focus on pictures for the story line and the sequence of events, which builds children's visual skills. In time, the "visually literate" child will find it easier to develop verbal and written skills.

Because a wordless folktale book is not restricted by reading ability or educational level, it can be used as a tool in helping children and adults, both English and non-English speakers, as well as readers and nonreaders to understand or retell a story from their own rich, ethnic perspective. Listening to folktales told on an audiocassette or in person offers another advantage; it allows the listener, who may be restricted by reading limitations, to enjoy literature, learn about other cultures, and develop essential prereading skills. Furthermore, it gives them confidence to retell stories on their own and motivates them to learn to read them.

Something special happens when you tell a story; something special happens when you hear a story well-told. Storytelling is a unique, entertaining, and powerful art form, one that creates an intimate bond between storyteller and listener, past and present. To take a story and give it a new voice is an exhilarating experience; to watch someone else take that same story and make it his or her own is another.

Janice M. Del Negro
Children's Services
The Chicago Public Library

The following story is a modern African American urban tale about two girls who compete in an after-school double dutch jump-rope contest to prove who is the best jumper. The presence of a secret helper and the delightful effect she has on a pair of shoes adds to the charm of this school yard tale.

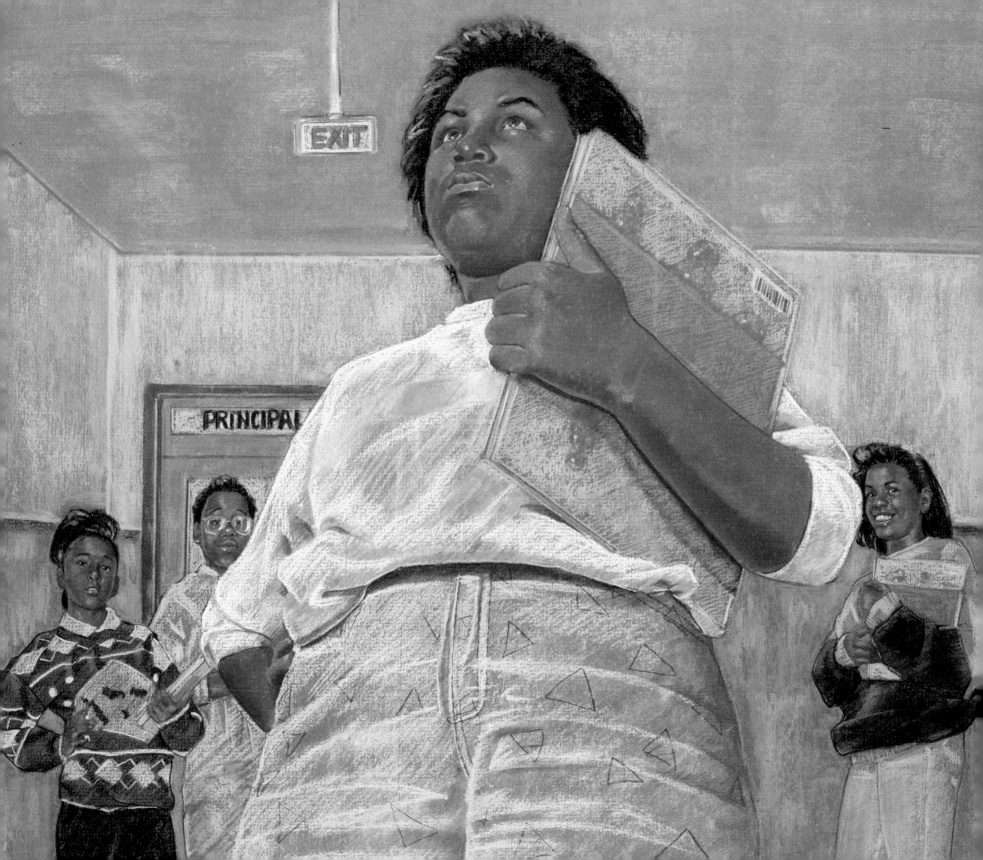

Story text

There's no one that can double dutch as good as Shalesea. Uh, uh. That girl is the best double dutcher in our whole school. She just jumps and jumps. She doesn't ever miss. And if you don't stop, Shalesea doesn't stop. You could be turning till your arms drop off.

Shalesea has been the best double dutcher ever since first grade. There's no one that can beat Shalesea. You look at Shalesea's feet when she's jumping and they're like one of those commercials on T.V. where everything's all blurry. You can't see how tiny her feet are.

Shalesea's had the same shoes ever since kindergarten. They're a pair of old blue and white keds. They've got holes in the top of them and holes in the bottom of them. When we were in third grade the soles of those old shoes started flopping around. But Shalesea didn't throw out the shoes. She got some old silver tape from the True Value hardware store and taped the tops and bottoms together.

There's no one that can beat Shalesea. But that was before Mayvelline transferred in. Mayvelline said that she was the best double dutcher on the westside and on the southside, and nobody could beat her. We just laughed and told her, "You haven't seen Shalesea double dutch." That afternoon, Mayvelline went out onto the playground to watch Shalesea. After we were done, Mayvelline walked over and said, "Hey, girl, I want to buy your shoes."

Shalesea just laughed at her. She said, "Ha! What do you want with my little old keds. They won't fit those gunboats you've got sticking out of your ankles."

Well, Mayvelline didn't give up. She just said, "I don't want to buy your shoes to wear them, I want them because I think they're what makes you so good. You aren't good at double dutch. It's your shoes. I suspect they've got some kind of voodoo in them."

We all started laughing at Mayvelline and thought, "Ha, voodoo, in Shalesea's old keds." But Shalesea wasn't laughing. She said, "I could beat you even without my good-luck jumping shoes." Mayvelline said, "All right, I challenge you to a game of double dutch. But you can't wear your keds, and I'll see you after school out on the playground."

Well, don't you know, we were all going to come to see that. When school was over, we all went out on the playground. Mayvelline got there first, and then Shalesea. And she brought her old keds with her. Mayvelline turned around and said, "Girl, I told you that you couldn't bring those keds." Shalesea said, "You said I couldn't wear them, you didn't say I couldn't bring them! I'm just going to put them down right here." And she asked me to watch them.

Just then the girls started turning the ropes. Mayvelline jumped in just as sweet as you please—and that girl was good. I've never seen anybody double dutch like that. She was flying! I looked over to where Shalesea's keds were supposed to be and they were gone. Before I could look back, Mayvelline said, "Ooo—Ouch!" And she fell down on the ground.

Then she turned around and said, "Somebody kicked me. Somebody kicked me right here twice." Shalesea just laughed and said, "Why girl, nobody kicked you. We've all been right here." Mayvelline said, "No, somebody kicked me." Everybody just laughed and said that Mayvelline was making it all up.

Then I turned around and saw Shalesea's keds walking over all by themselves. They started jumping and dancing like they were real happy about something. There were two little scuff marks right on the top of the silver tape.

Well, Shalesea started jumping rope. She beat Mayvelline's 230 double dutches real easy. Now, I know what I saw. I know I saw those shoes moving all by themselves. But every time I try to tell somebody, they say I'm just making it up. And Shalesea, well, you know she isn't talking.

Now if you don't believe me, that's all right. But you come down to my playground at 16th and Central Park and challenge Shalesea to a game of double dutch. You'll see for yourself!

Project Editor: Alice Flanagan
Design and Electronic Page Composition: Biner Design
Engraver: Liberty Photoengravers

About the storyteller

My name is Donna Lanette Washington. I am the story-teller you hear on the tape recording of *Double Dutch and the Voodoo Shoes*. I also am one of the characters in the story. The illustrator of this book has drawn me as Shalesea's spirit helper.

I have loved stories ever since I was very young. Every night at dinnertime, during dessert, my father would sit at the head of the table and tell stories. That was when I discovered that I could travel around the world and through time without ever leaving my chair.

When I began college at Northwestern University, the world of storytelling was reopened for me. Once again I could feel the magic of stories. It was at this time that I decided to bring the magic to others.

Since I graduated, I have shared many stories with many people. I hope you have enjoyed hearing the story about Shalesea's special shoes and will want to share it with others.

Donna L. Washington

About the illustrator

My name is Melodye Rosales. I live in Champaign, Illinois, with my husband and two children, Dino and Harmony. As an African-American artist, it gives me great joy to share my talent with an audience that I understand so well. It took many years to learn my craft. Although no artist ever perfects his or her talent within one lifetime, it is exciting to try.

I have always been a daydreamer. Like most children growing up, I surrounded myself with fantasy — creating characters that I would draw over and over again in different stories. Much later, as an adult, it seemed quite natural for me to pursue a career as a children's book illustrator.

Double Dutch and the Voodoo Shoes was a challenge to illustrate. Before beginning to draw the characters in the story, I watched children jumping rope. I photographed the girls who looked most like the book characters as I imagined them. Afterward, I drew preliminary sketches from the photographs. I found that taking photos of real people helped me to remember actual features and realistic expressions.

Melodye Angelo Rosales

Storytelling activities

Storytelling provides a wonderful opportunity to share information, feelings, and a love of books with children. Some of the following activities may be helpful in making this possible:

🍃 Ask children to retell the story. This will help you measure their comprehension and interact with them through quiet conversation.

🍃 Have paper and magic markers or crayons available so children can draw the story. You might ask them to draw a picture of one of the characters in the book or make a story map (a series of drawings reflecting the sequence of story events).

🍃 Ask children to tell the story from different points of view. Have them retell the story several times — each time basing it on the viewpoint of a different character.

More about storytelling and folktales

If you'd like to read more about storytelling or other stories with African-American characters, check out some of the following books from your local library:

Breneman, Lucille N. and Bren. *Once Upon a Time: A Storytelling Handbook*. Chicago: Nelson-Hall, 1983.

Sierra, Judy. *Twice Upon a Time: Stories to Tell, Retell, Act Out and Write About*. New York: H. W. Wilson, 1989.

Cameron, Ann. *Stories Julian Tells*. New York: Pantheon, 1981.

Greenfield, Eloise. *Nathaniel Talking*. New York: Black Butterfly Children's Books, 1989.

Humphrey, Margo. *The River that Gave Gifts*. Emeryville, CA: Children's Book Press, 1987.

Ringgold, Faith. *Tar Beach*. New York: Crown, 1991.

Library of Congress Cataloging-in- Publication Data
Rosales, Melodye.
        Double dutch and the voodoo shoes : an urban folktale / illustrated by Melodye Rosales.
           p.   cm.— (Adventures in storytelling)
        Includes bibliographical references.
        Summary: Two girls compete in a double dutch jump rope contest to prove who is the best jumper. Includes storytelling activities and a list of books on storytelling and folktales.
        ISBN 0-516-05133-4
        [1. Rope skipping — Fiction. 2. Contests — Fiction. 3. Afro-Americans — Fiction.]
I. Title. II. Series.
PZ7.R7138Do 1991
[E] — dc20
                                        91-13153
                                        CIP
                                        AC

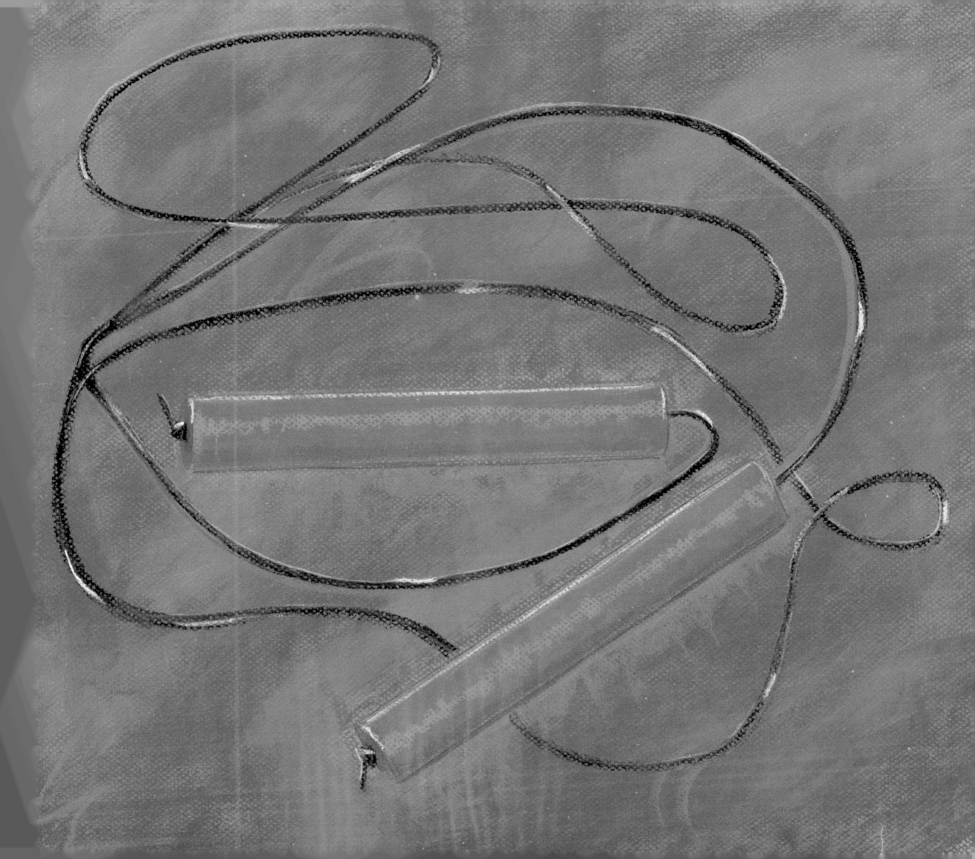